FUN FACT!

You can get more Awesome Dog
in these adventures!

#1 *Awesome Dog 5000*

#2 *Awesome Dog 5000 vs.
Mayor Bossypants*

#3 *Awesome Dog 5000 vs.
the Kitty-Cat Cyber Squad*

AWESOME DOG 5000

5000

vs. THE KITTY-CAT CYBER SQUAD

JUSTIN DEAN

Random House New York

All rights reserved. Published in the United States by Random House Children's Books, a division of Penguin Random House LLC, New York.

Random House and the colophon are registered trademarks of Penguin Random House LLC.

Photo p.169 by Dmitry Kalinovsky/Shutterstock.com

Visit us on the Web! rhcbooks.com

Educators and librarians, for a variety of teaching tools, visit us at RHTeachersLibrarians.com

Library of Congress Cataloging-in-Publication Data
Name: Dean, Justin, author.
Title: Awesome Dog 5000 vs. the Kitty-Cat Cyber Squad / Justin Dean.
Other titles: Awesome Dog 5000 Versus the Kitty-Cat Cyber Squad
Description: First edition. | New York: Random House Children's Books, [2021] | Series: Awesome Dog 5000 ; 3 | Summary: "Marty, Ralph, and Skyler create their own superhero personas, while Awesome Dog's biggest fan becomes Townville's newest supervillain and creates a team of robot kittens that challenge the robot dog in his most dangerous battle yet"—Provided by publisher.
Identifiers: LCCN 2020005845 (print) | LCCN 2020005846 (ebook) | ISBN 978-0-593-17282-7 (trade) | ISBN 978-0-593-17284-1 (lib. bdg.) | ISBN 978-0-593-17283-4 (ebook)
Subjects: CYAC: Robots—Fiction. | Dogs—Fiction. | Cats—Fiction. | Adventure and adventurers—Fiction. | Superheroes—Fiction. | Supervillains—Fiction. | Science fiction.
Classification: LCC PZ7.1.D3985 Awj 2020 (print) | LCC PZ7.1.D3985 (ebook) | DDC [Fic]—dc23

The artist used iPad Pro with Apple Pencil, Procreate by Savage Interactive, and Adobe Photoshop to create the illustrations for this book. The text of this book is set in 12-point Caecilia.

Printed in the United States of America
10 9 8 7 6 5 4 3 2 1
First Edition

This one's for Mom—you taught me to write,
to draw, and to always believe in myself.
I owe all these words and pictures to you.

CHAPTER 1

A New Sheriff in Town

IT IS THE YEAR 3003, and the galaxy is at peace.

After a long and brutal war, the army of alien slime ninjas has finally been defeated. Their last remaining leader, Commander Smooshy-butt, has surrendered and sent a muffin basket as an apology. Earth has been saved, and it's all thanks to the bravest hero in the universe. He is . . .

SHERIFF TURBO-KARATE!

And he really needs a break from all the space fighting. So he's going on vacation in Florida. He's trading in his rocket boots for flip-flops and chilling on the beach with a mango smoothie. Now he's . . .

BEACH DUDE TURBO-KARATE!

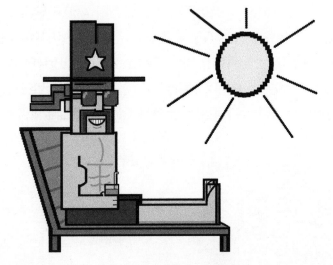

OR what if he doesn't go to Florida—he moves to Canada. He grows a beard, buys a flannel shirt, and installs a syrup dispenser in his cowboy hat. Now he's . . .

LUMBERJACK TURBO-KARATE!

OR maybe he doesn't do either of those things. Instead, he goes to the park and is bitten by a radioactive caterpillar. He grows giant colorful wings and sprouts long antennae. He uses his infinity fart attack to toot flowery smells. Now he's . . .

BUTTERFLY TURBO-KARATE!

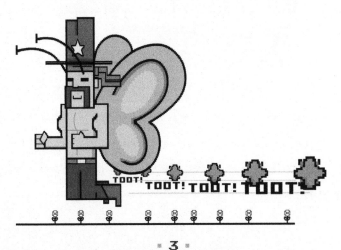

TOOT! TOOT! TOOT! TOOT!

A ten-inch-tall bug-man flapped his wings as green gas puffed out of his backside. It created a stinky haze in the design lab. The doll was one of three robotic action figures displayed on pedestals.

A tall, slender woman was remote-controlling the doll with a handheld gizmo. She coughed and waved away the gas. "Sorry about the stench. I'm still working on getting it to smell more like lavender and less like moldy cheese. My programming keeps going haywire for some reason," she said.

The woman was wearing a lab coat and neon-green glasses. There was an ID badge clipped to her coat.

Tina was showing off the prototypes to her boss, Takashi Videomoto. He was president of the world-renowned video game company Funstation. The Japanese company had recently expanded its business by building a toy factory. It was going to make action figures based on the star of its most popular game, *Sheriff Turbo-Karate*.

Tina hadn't followed the business plan.

"I hired you to make a new Sheriff Turbo-Karate doll. Not a new *version* of Sheriff Turbo-Karate," said Mr. Videomoto.

Tina explained, "Yes, but I thought we should try something different. You always do the same boring 'Sheriff Turbo-Karate fights blob aliens' thing. That's, like, the *exact* same idea you've used twice already for the video games." Tina beamed a smile. "Who doesn't love a new hero, right?"

"Me," snapped Mr. Videomoto. He walked down the line of pedestals, scrutinizing each model.

"I want the original Sheriff Turbo-Karate. No sunglasses. No flannel. And definitely no fart bugs."

Tina gave an embarrassed nod.

"Get rid of all this and start over," demanded Mr. Videomoto. "I'll be back in two weeks to check your progress. And crack a window—it smells terrible in here."

Tina dumped the three prototypes into the trash and, as ordered, opened a window. That was when she heard a series of loud pops and bangs outside. There was a bizarre daytime fireworks show with geysers of water followed by screams of terror. Tina sprinted out of the factory to see what had happened.

She ran down the block and rounded the corner. It was an event for the city's mayor. Mayor

Bossypants had constructed a hundred-foot-tall statue of himself, but the statue celebration had gone horribly wrong. It was chaos. Hundreds of people soaked in water were trying to escape deafening rock music, laser lights, and terrifying giant holograms.

Somebody cried out, "Help me!"

Tina looked up to see a man in a jumpsuit hanging from the top of the statue. The man sneezed. His hand slipped, and he fell from the statue. And then, out of nowhere, a blinding white streak swooped in and caught the man. He was flown off to safety.

Tina turned to a guy next to her and said, "Oh my gadgets! Did you see that? TELL ME YOU SAW THAT! A flying robot dog just rescued that guy. I have to know everything about this new hero!"

And that is a fantastic transition to the "Guide to Awesome Dog 5000." I couldn't have planned that better myself, and I'm the book!

GUIDE TO
AWESOME DOG 5000:
HOME PAGE

To improve your Awesome Dog 5000 reading experience, we've created four custom options to get you up to speed with the story. Choose your speed accordingly, and proceed to the page indicated.*

THE "SPAM THE ATTACK BUTTON" OPTION:

You've recently finished the first two books in the Awesome Dog 5000 series, and you are ready

---

* Disclaimer: While readers are free to explore any option, you probably shouldn't choose option 4. That snail is legendary. You will lose every time.

to zoom straight into the next adventure. Please turn to page 18.

THE "WELCOME TO THE ZEROES CLUB" OPTION:

You've read the first two books, but a quick refresher would help. Please turn to page 13.

THE "THINK FOUND DOG" OPTION:

You randomly picked up this book and started reading it without any clue what an Awesome Dog 5000 is. Please turn to page 12.

THE "SNAIL SQUAD 4 LIFE" OPTION:

You got this book because you love the Snail Squad and want to read more about them—and only them. You don't care about any of this Awesome Dog 5000 stuff. To skip over everything in the book and have fun battling a snail in a staring contest, please turn to page 206.

THE "THINK FOUND DOG" OPTION

Thanks for randomly discovering this book! Now go randomly find the first and second books. Read them both, and then turn to the next page.

THE "WELCOME TO THE ZEROES CLUB" OPTION

Welcome back! It's so great to see you again, reader. How have you been? I've just been, ya know, hanging out on the shelf, being papery.

But enough about me. This is a recap about everything Awesome Dog 5000! Well, not *everything*. It's the highlights. We're going to gloss over a few things like exploding mansions, the queen of England monster, and that butler named Mr. Poopsie.

Before we get to Awesome Dog, we should start with these three:

MARTY FONTANA	RALPH ROGERS	SKYLER KWON
●NEW KID IN TOWN	●NEVER COMBS HAIR	● SKATEBOARD PUNK
●WEARS RED HIGH-TOPS	●VERY SMART	● DAREDEVIL
●NAMED THE SCHOOL'S BIGGEST DORK	●BLURTS OUT RANDOM FUN FACTS	● LISTENS TO WEIRDO ROCK MUSIC

Marty, Ralph, and Skyler were best friends who did everything together, including playing their handheld Funstations in co-op mode. Their favorite video game was *Sheriff Turbo-Karate,* and they couldn't wait to save up their money and get the sequel, *Sheriff Turbo-Karate 2: Gold Deluxe Edition.*

When they weren't gaming, the Zeroes Club members were hanging with Awesome Dog 5000, or Fives, as he's nick-named. He was loaded with all sorts of cool gadgets, from rocket paws to

a mega-cannon. Since finding him, the kids had put his equipment to good use by stopping bad guys.

One such bad guy was the city's former mayor, Mr. Bossypants. He had built a statue of himself and thrown an extravagant party to convince the world he was "epic." The party was a total disaster—the same disaster you read about in the first chapter.

Mayor Bossypants had been so humiliated, he created a giant mech-suit. He was going to prove his epicness by taking over the entire world. However, Awesome Dog and the kids foiled his plan. They defeated him in a big junkyard battle by stripping off his armor and left him in his underwear, crying like a baby.

When Awesome Dog dropped the mayor off at jail, a few people took some blurry photos and shaky videos. Now everyone wanted to know who the city's new superheroes were.

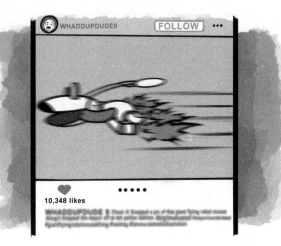

Besides saving the day and keeping their identities a secret, the kids were also trying to solve the mystery of Awesome Dog's origins. Fives had been left behind by the previous owner of Marty's house, a strange toothbrush inventor.

The kids had no idea where the inventor was, but they had discovered his secret workshop under Fives's doghouse (that they then converted into the Zeroes Club headquarters, HQ0). And just when it couldn't get any stranger, the kids received a secret coded message in the mail:

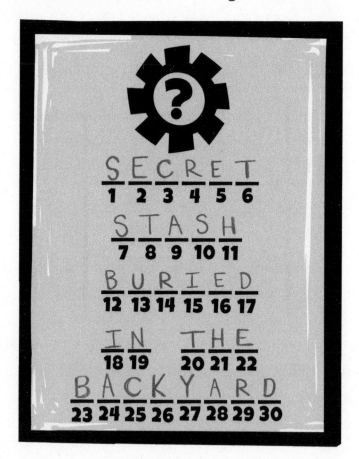

Which is exactly why the Zeroes Club and Awesome Dog were at Marty's house right now . . .

CHAPTER 2

The Secret Stash

"FUN FACT!" SAID RALPH. "A teenager in New Mexico once found a ten-thousand-year-old asteroid in the sand with one of these things."

"It feels like we've been out *here* for ten thousand years," groaned Skyler. "Maybe it's broken."

Marty waved a metal detector over the grass. The Zeroes Club had borrowed it from Ralph's garage. They hoped it would locate the buried secret stash.

"It works. We just haven't found the right spot yet," said Marty.

The kids had spent all afternoon scanning the back-yard. There had been a steady hiss of static. Nothing had set off a signal.

"BARK. BARK. SWITCHING FROM SOLAR POWER TO

RESERVE BATTERY," said Awesome Dog. His eye lights clicked on as the sun went down.

"It's time we go with plan B," said Skyler. "We dig up the entire backyard. No stone unturned. No worm kicked out of its house."

"Does the 'B' in your plan B stand for 'bonkers'?" asked Marty. "Because my mom will lose it if we do that. We already blew up her front yard with a missile last month."

Ralph held up a finger. "And we all learned a valuable lesson that day: always be careful when playing fetch with Awesome Dog."

Marty pulled the "secret message" certificate from a pocket of his shorts. The header on the gold paper was a gear emblem with a question mark in its center. He reread the message aloud: "'Secret stash buried in the backyard.' Hmm. There's got to be more to this puzzle."

Marty squinted. All this mystery stuff was giving him a stress headache. He rubbed his temples with his thumbs.

"Hey, what if we do plan C," offered Ralph. "We call off the search for the night, and we 'C' if we can figure this out tomorrow with fresh eyes."

Skyler jumped in on the plan. "Yeah. You guys can come over to my house for dinner. My dad can make us his special kimchi pizza again."

Marty didn't respond. He didn't even turn around. It wasn't because he didn't like Mr. Kwon's cooking. He was focused on something else. His head was cocked to the side as he stared at a nearby tree.

"What's he doing?" Skyler asked Ralph.

"Seeing something with fresh eyes," said Marty. "There wasn't anything else to the puzzle. We were just trying to solve it at the wrong time of day."

He pointed to the tree trunk. There was a green gear with a question mark in the center. It was written in glow-in-the-dark paint!

CHAPTER 3

Gear Marks the Spot

THE KIDS HAD FOUND WHERE the secret stash was buried, but shovels wouldn't be needed. They had their very own heavy-duty excavator.

Marty pointed to the base of the tree with the gear emblem. "Fives, dig here!"

"BARK. BARK. ARCHAEOLOGY MODE ACTIVATED," said Awesome Dog.

The robot dog's wrists began rotating like two drills. There was a whirring *zzzzzzzzz* sound as they spun faster. Fives pressed his paws to the grass and burrowed under the tree. He emerged, covered in dirt, a few feet away. In his mouth he was carrying a case by its handle.

Ralph took the case from Awesome Dog and tapped on the hard plastic exterior. "Explains why the metal detector didn't get a signal," he said.

The side of the case was marked: BEWARE! CONTENTS ARE

EXTREMELY POWERFUL. USE WITH CAUTION.

The top was covered in warning stickers: HIGH VOLT-AGE, EXPLOSIVE, TOXIC, RADIO-ACTIVE, FLAMMABLE, and even a TOO MANY WARNING STICK-ERS warning sticker. Whatever was inside the secret stash was dangerous.

Marty took a step back.

Ralph nervously bit his bottom lip.

Skyler's jaw dropped.

Then she let out a giddy laugh. She yelled,

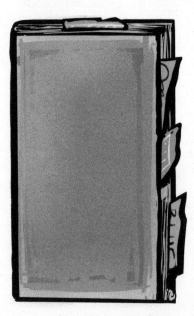

"JACKPOT!" as she grabbed the case from Ralph and pried it open. But her smile quickly faded. Inside was a thick leather-bound book.

And that was it.

"That better be a book of magic spells that summons zombies with eye lasers or something, or I am going to be *very* dis-appointed," said Skyler.

Marty opened the book. The top half of the first page had been torn out. There was the tail end of a handwritten entry: "—just follow the directions."

"It's some kind of diary," said Marty.

"Better be a wizard's diary," muttered Skyler.

They thumbed through the pages. There were scribbled notes, advanced equations, chemical mixtures, machine schematics, a map of the city, computer coding, some—

"Wait a second," said Ralph. "I've seen that before." He flipped back to a diagram of a cylinder attached to a bent pole. "Do you two realize what this is?"

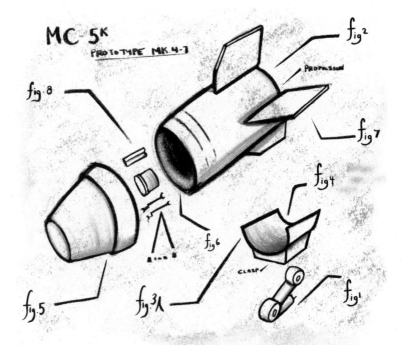

MC-5ᴷ
PROTOTYPE MK.4-7

f_{ig}8
f_{ig}2
PROPULSION
f_{ig}7
f_{ig}4
f_{ig}6
CLASP
f_{ig}5
f_{ig}3λ
f_{ig}1

Marty guessed, "A fancy thermos holder?"

"Activate mega-cannon!" ordered Ralph.

"BARK. BARK. ACTIVATING ATOMIC MEGA-CANNON," said Fives. The hatch on his back opened. The metal arm that folded out held a cylindrical missile.

"This book isn't just a diary. This is the diary of the guy who created Fives," said Ralph. "We've got the blueprints for all his inventions."

Marty looked to Skyler and asked, "Still disappointed?"

CHAPTER 4

Tina Tinkerwith, Superfan

TOWNVILLE WAS OBSESSED with the new superhero they had dubbed "Amazing Pup."

Each new sighting of the dog and his friends made front-page news. All the sandwich shops changed their menus to list only "hero" sub sandwiches. Stores exclusively sold Amazing Pup merchandise. The shelves were stocked

with themed hats, mugs, and Puppy Power! energy drink. Amazing Pup was an instant celebrity!

Amazing Pup—I mean, Awesome Dog—had a lot of admirers, but without a doubt his number one fan was Tina Tinkerwith. Being a fangirl wasn't new for Tina. She had always been fascinated by tales of daring courage and acts of bravery. As a kid, she'd constantly watched superhero movies and read comics, but her favorite thing

NOW WITH 24 KARAT KICK MOVE

DIAMOND DANGER

SHE'S TOUGH
SHE'S BRIGHT
SHE'S A SHINING JEWEL OF JUSTICE

to do was to play with action figures. She had a toy box full of caped musclemen and magical women in shiny boots. She would stay in her room for hours playing pretend.

Tina really enjoyed coming up with elaborate scenarios where her heroic toys had to save a rubber ducky from drowning in the tub, or the action figures were pitted against the evil mastermind Baby Doll. Tina loved her superhero toys so much that she wanted to play with them forever. So she decided to become a toy inventor. The job combined her creativity with her sharp intellect.

She had been hired at Funstation to create a Sheriff Turbo-Karate action figure. Her three robotic prototypes were beautifully detailed, technological marvels . . . and not at all what her boss wanted.

When she was given a second chance, an

opportunity to fix the mistake, Mr. Videomoto was shocked by the results.

"Nothing?!" he exclaimed.

"Mr. Videomoto, I've been really busy lately," Tina said, holding up scissors and a bottle of glue. She had wasted the past two weeks crafting an enormous Amazing Pup collage. She had cut out and pasted together thousands of magazine and newspaper photos of the robot dog onto a poster board. Every picture had lipstick kisses.

"You've been smooching on the job!" yelled Mr. Videomoto. "You're fired!"

Tina pleaded to keep her job, but Mr. Videomoto shook his head and pointed to the exit. There was nothing more she could do. Her lifelong dream of being a toy inventor was over.

Tina was heartbroken, but it wasn't all bad. She could now spend time adding glitter to her collage. She packed up her desk plant, her cat-of-the-month calendar, and her poster. Tina had planned on showing off the collage at the Thumbs-Up on Saving Townville ceremony. The

city was holding a celebration for its new super-hero. It would also accidentally create its next supervillain.

But we'll get around to that part a little later, in chapter 10.

CHAPTER 5

Morning Announcements

FROM THE MOMENT THE KIDS dug up the inventor's journal, Ralph couldn't put it down. There were hundreds of blueprints, for everything from a grappling-hook pen for writing on the go to a motorcycle that used a combination of root beer and ice cream as fuel. It was called

the float-orcycle. Ralph read the book cover to cover. Then he read it again.

He was rereading the diary in Mrs. Taylor's class when Marty sat down at the desk next to him. "I thought you'd have that memorized by now, Ralph. Find anything cool?"

"Kinda, I guess," said Ralph. "I wouldn't even know what to do with most of this stuff. It's all so random. Check this one out." The page showed a timer attached to massive stereo speakers. "It's an alarm clock that wakes you up with a blast of sound so loud it blows you out of bed."

"What happens when you hit the snooze button, a boxing glove to the face?" joked Marty.

The speaker on the classroom wall squawked. It was time for announcements.

The principal's voice came through the speaker. "Attention, students! It's spirit week at

Nikola Tesla Elementary. Please show your pride by wearing a T-shirt with our school mascot, Linus the Lightning Bug, on it. In the cafeteria, lunches will be fried 'food' chunks, last week's sloppy joes, grayish-green casserole, and corn. For athletics, the after-school basketball team is now open for sign-ups."

"We gotta do that," Marty said to Ralph. Basketball was easily Marty's favorite sport.

The principal continued. "Lastly, tomorrow will be a half day so that everyone can attend the Thumbs-Up on Saving Townville event in the park. Our newly elected mayor, Gal Goodlady, has extended an invitation to Amazing Pup and his team of sidekicks. At the ceremony she'll award them the title of our city's official heroes. Best of all, the event is guaranteed to be free of any giant holograms or terrifying fireworks, like our last mayor's celebration. That is the end of the announcements. Have a great school day!"

Ralph leaned over to Marty and whispered, "Holy moon cheese. They're making us official heroes."

Marty shook his head. "No, no, no. We are not accepting that invitation, Ralph. Eject the thought right out of your big brain. It's way too risky. We'd have to reveal our secret identities."

"C'mon, we have to go!" pleaded Ralph.

To decide whether or not to attend, Marty and Ralph came to an agreement. They'd both make a list of reasons they should or should not expose their secret identities to get the award. Marty would write all the negatives. Ralph would write all the positives. Whoever had the longer list would be the one to decide. This was what they came up with:

MARTY'S LIST

1. BAD GUYS WILL KNOW OUR REAL NAMES

2. BAD GUYS WILL KNOW WHERE WE LIVE

3. BAD GUYS WILL GET REVENGE ON US

4. OUR PARENTS WILL BE IN DANGER FROM BAD GUY ATTACKS

5. OUR NEIGHBORS WILL BE IN DANGER FROM BAD GUY ATTACKS

6. OUR MAILMAN WILL BE IN DANGER FROM BAD GUY ATTACKS

7. WE WILL BE LIVING IN CONSTANT FEAR OF BAD GUY ATTACKS

8. PUBLIC SPEAKING IS SCARY

RALPH'S LIST

it'll be fun

It was obvious. The Zeroes Club definitely should not attend the celebration. However, when the boys met up with Skyler for lunch in the cafeteria, she proposed a third option. They could keep their secret identities *and* go to the event.

"Costumes," she said.

Marty asked, "Costumes? What're you talking about?"

Skyler made circles with her fingers and thumbs and held them to her eyes. "I'm talking about masks. I'm talking about capes. I'm talking about an after-school fashion show!"

CHAPTER 6

Laundry Day

COATS, SHIRTS, PANTS, SCARVES, sunglasses, tights, and socks were scattered across the HQ0 floor. The three kids had raided every closet in their houses. They had spent hours mixing and matching options to create the perfect outfits.

"Dut-duh-dah! It's Super Awesome!" announced Marty.

Marty stood confidently with his hands on

his hips. He was wearing winter gloves and a tank top with the letter "A" written in marker across the front. He had a black bandanna over his face, with holes cut out for his eyes. A small red blanket was tied around his neck, like a cape. The cape blew in the wind.

It wasn't really wind. They were in an underground room without any windows. Awesome Dog just had his rocket paws raised and was blowing out steam.

Next, Skyler rode out into the center of the room on her skateboard. She had on a dirt bike chest protector and purple leggings. She was sporting her dad's snowboarding goggles and wore her hair in a ponytail.

"And I'm Purple Lightning!" she said.

"Looking sharp, Purple Lightning," Marty said. "We make quite the team."

"Almost a team. Ralph, let's see how you look!" shouted Skyler.

Ralph had changed clothes in the HQ0 storage closet and was nervous to show off his costume. Marty and Skyler had cool names and outfits. Ralph had on a tattered ski mask and a T-shirt he thought made his belly stand out. Without his hoodie, Ralph felt exposed. He didn't like clothes that showed his body shape. He slouched with his arms wrapped over his stomach. Finally, he put on a fake smile and walked out.

"Hello. I'm the, uh, Brain Thinker, or maybe I could go with Fact Person," mumbled Ralph. He lowered his eyes and shrugged. "Captain Mind-Guy . . . or something."

Marty was quick to offer a suggestion. "What about . . ." He swiped a marker, pulled the cap off with his teeth, and wrote two letters on the forehead of Ralph's ski mask. "I.Q., Professor I.Q."

Ralph smiled. This time he wasn't faking. He liked the name, but he wasn't completely confident yet. Skyler noticed that Ralph was covering up his midsection. She snapped her fingers and said, "Your costume is really good, but I think we can make it great."

She searched through the piles of clothes until she found a short-sleeved button-up shirt and a bow tie. She dressed up Ralph. His costume now made him kind of resemble a real professor—or at least a professor of skiing. Ralph dropped his arms to his sides and stood up straight. Skyler hadn't made him feel great. She'd made him feel super.

"BARK. BARK. TEAM AWESOME ASSEMBLED," said Awesome Dog.

Marty smirked and said, "Let's go make it official."

CHAPTER 7

Townville's Official Celebration

THE MASSIVE CROWD CHANTED, "A-maze-ing Pup! A-maze-ing Pup! A-maze-ing Pup!"

The Thumbs-Up on Saving Townville celebration was so loud that Skyler, Marty, and Ralph could hear it from a thousand feet up in the sky. They were flying toward the city park on Awesome Dog's leash.

"There's the stage," said Marty. He pointed to the platform below. It was decorated with a big welcome banner and balloons. "Take us down nice and easy, Skyler."

"Where's the fun in that?" she asked.

Skyler was piloting Fives with the customized Funstation controller plugged into his leash. She mashed the up button and rolled her thumb clockwise on the directional pad. Awesome Dog

took off high into the air, then twirled back down in a figure eight. Team Awesome stuck the landing with a THWOOMP! center stage. The crowd went wild with applause.

"We're rock stars!" said Ralph.

Mayor Goodlady formally introduced them. "Citizens of Townville, I am proud to welcome Amazing Pup and his friends!"

Skyler leaned into the mayor's microphone and corrected her. "Actually, he's called Awesome Dog 5000."

The crowd started a new chant: "Awe-some Dog! Awe-some Dog! Awe-some Dog!"

Everyone was extra-pumped to learn this new information. Everyone except Fred, the owner of Fred's Amazing Pup Gift Shop. He was extra-sad.

His store and all his merchandise now had the wrong name.

"I'm Purple Lightning," said Skyler. "These are Super Awesome and Professor I.Q., and we are Team Awesome."

Way in the back, a woman yelled out, "We love you, Team Awesome!"

It was Tina Tinkerwith. She held up her collage, but she was too far away from the stage for the kids to see it.

"Team Awesome, in gratitude for saving the city from a super-villain, we'd like to present to you these medals of courage!" said Mayor Goodlady.

She placed the awards around their necks. The gold medals were engraved with the city's seal and the words CITY OF TOWNVILLE OFFICIAL HERO.

The mayor extended the mic and asked, "Would any of you like to say something to your fans?"

Marty waved his hands in front of him. He was terrified of public speaking. Ralph wasn't so shy. He blurted out, "Fun fact! Gold is one of the rare metals that are odorless and tasteless." He sniffed the medal. Then he licked it. Then he spit on the ground and gagged. "Blurk! Gold plastic, however, does have a taste. An incredibly yucky taste!"

A hush fell over the crowd. Superheroes

tended not to almost puke in front of their fans. Ralph tried to cover. "Fun fact! Humans drink about six cups of their own spit a day!"

A crowd of disgusted faces stared back at Ralph. He had made the situation worse. A little girl said, "Ugh, Professor I.Q.'s gross, Mommy."

Ralph slunk away and hid behind Marty in embarrassment. Skyler quickly swiped the microphone. "I have something to say, and it doesn't involve licking things! We may be Townville's official heroes, but taking care of this city is a team effort, and that team is bigger than us. We're all in this together."

A few fans started clapping. Skyler kept the momentum going. "It's not just about stopping supervillains. It's about making the world a better place, one little step at a time. It could be donating a few bucks to a charity, or picking up litter on the sidewalk, or just saying 'please' and 'thank you' more often. It's the small things added up that make a big difference. There's a hero in all of us—you just have to figure out how you can help in your own way."

The crowd roared with cheers. The mayor held up a piece of paper and said, "As the mayor, I want to set an example of how we all can help! Here is my extra-special 'Get Anything You Want for Free' coupon! What would you like to use it on, Team Awesome?"

"You're going to give us anything we want for free?" asked Marty.

The choice was obvious. The three kids said in unison, *"Sheriff Turbo-Karate 2: Gold Deluxe Edition!"*

Skyler's speech had inspired the crowd, but it was the kids' request for Sheriff Turbo-Karate that sparked a new idea in Tina's head. She decided she was going to help the city of Townville in her own way. Tina was going to use her skills as a toymaker to create a brand-new robotic sidekick for Awesome Dog.

CHAPTER 8

The Purr-fect Idea

TINA LEFT THE CELEBRATION early and went back to the workshop in her garage. She was eager to start making her robotic sidekick. She unrolled a fresh sheet of paper across her drafting table, sharpened a pencil, and set a fire extinguisher by her feet. She knew she'd have so many ideas the paper might ignite from the speed of her drawing.

She dabbed the pencil lead to her tongue and began to . . . sit there. Her mind was completely blank. Tina had the idea to make a robot sidekick, but no idea what kind of robot to make. It was an awful case of inventor's block. She stared at the page for a long time. Like, a really long time. The sun went down, came up, then went down again. She was stumped for so long, she lost track of what day it was. She checked the date on her cat-of-the-month calendar.

"OH MY GADGETS! THAT'S IT!" Tina knew exactly what kind of robot to make. "Of course! It was so obvious," she said.

Tina furiously scribbled out a blueprint, slowing down only when her pencil started smoking. She gazed at her finished sketch with pride. The new sidekick prototype was going to be a ROBO-CALENDAR!

"Hmm. Maybe it's not that obvious," she said. Tina looked back at the cat calendar. She quickly revised her plans. The new sidekick prototype was going to be a ROBO-CAT!

Tina cut, welded, and installed machine parts into a small feline frame. The prototype had a raw, unfinished look. There were exposed sections of its body plating, and its eyes were two lightbulbs. The crudely made robo-cat had been

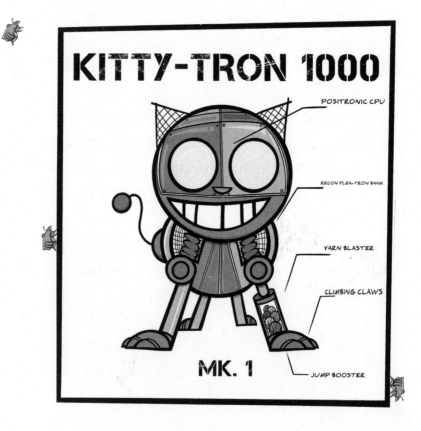

KITTY-TRON 1000

POSITRONIC CPU

RECON FLEA-TRON BANK

YARN BLASTER

CLIMBING CLAWS

JUMP BOOSTER

MK. 1

programmed to be a helper bot and was equipped with an assortment of features.

Tina wound the key on the cat's back. The motor inside rumbled. One of its eyes lit up. Tina gave a few bangs on its head until the second eye flickered on.

"MEOW. MEOW. I AM KITTY-TRON 1000, YOUR FRIENDLY ROBOT ASSISTANT. HOW MAY I HELP YOU TODAY?" asked the robo-cat.

"Let's do a test run. I want to find some people we can help," said Tina.

"MEOW. MEOW. LAUNCHING FLEA-TRON SEARCH," said the kitty-tron.

A slot on the back of its collar opened and deployed an army of micro-bots. They were no bigger than a speck of rice, each with six legs and a little blinking dot on its back. They were the flea-trons, designed to seek out any given target. The flea-trons scattered off in every direction. It didn't take long for them to radio back what they had found.

"MEOW. MEOW. FLEA-TRONS HAVE IDENTIFIED THREE POSSIBLE TARGETS TO HELP," said the robo-cat.

Tina put on her favorite Amazing Pup T-shirt

and took her robot cat downtown. They were off to save the day.

CHAPTER 9

The Kitty-tron Triple Play

TINA AND KITTY-TRON 1000 followed the flea-trons' signal downtown to a trio of people with three unique problems:

Across the street, a baby was crying. The dad pushing the stroller was holding an empty milk bottle.

In front of an apartment high-rise, four movers were unloading a grand piano from their delivery truck. The piano weighed a ton and was difficult for them to lift.

One of the movers said, "There's no way we're getting this thing up to apartment 815. That's on the eighth floor!"

At the curb, a timid old granny with a walker was waiting to cross the road.

Tina gave her orders. "Kitty-tron, bring the baby some milk, take that piano all the way up to apartment 815, and get the old woman to the other side of the road. Make it quick."

"MEOW. MEOW. HELP MODE ACTIVATED," said the robot cat.

The kitty-tron fired its jump boosters. The cat crashed through the side of All-Mart. It dropped into the dairy aisle, grabbed two gallons of milk, and then super-bounced over to the crying baby and her dad. The kitty-tron dumped both jugs of milk on their heads before leaping away to the delivery truck.

I AM HELPING!

The robot cat extended its claws and ripped the piano out of the movers' hands. The kitty-tron threw the piano at an open window on the eighth floor. The piano was too big to fit through it and shattered against the window frame.

Finally, the kitty-tron jumped over to the grandma. The robot cat raised its front legs and fired the yarn blasters in its paws. Multiple yarn balls struck the old woman in the back, pushing her across the street.

"EEEK!" squealed the grandma. She thought she was being attacked. This wasn't any typical grandma, though. She was Granny Nunchucks, a kung fu master. She ripped her walker apart and linked the metal bars together with her pearl neck-  lace. She had crafted her signature weapon.

The grandma cartwheeled toward the kittytron. She rounded it out with a nunchuck uppercut. The robot's head spun backward as it was launched into the sky and dropped at Tina's feet.

Tina surveyed the damage she had caused. A baby was doing the backstroke in a milk-filled stroller. Piano debris was scattered across the sidewalk. Worst of all, her robot sidekick was destroyed.

Tina carried the mangled kitty-tron to a dumpster in the alley. "So much for helping out Awesome Dog."

She was about to throw the kitty robot

away when someone said, "I wouldn't do that if I were you."

Tina turned around to see a man in a black cloak. His right hand was a mechanical claw.

CHAPTER 10

The Return of Mr. Clawhand

"AND WHO ARE YOU?" Tina asked.

The man in the cloak flashed a smile and said, "I'm just a concerned citizen trying to help out in my own way, like you." He pulled back his cloak to reveal his Amazing Pup T-shirt. It was the same

one Tina was wearing. "I was picking up litter with my claw hand when I saw your robot cat pour milk on that baby, smash the piano, and shove an old person. Purple Lightning said doing small things *can* make a big difference. Right?"

"The only thing I made was a mess," said Tina. She tossed the kitty-tron into the dumpster and walked off.

The man called out, "Ya know, there is more than one way to help a superhero."

Tina stopped in her tracks. She was curious.

"Allow me to properly introduce myself," the man said. He drew a business card out from under his cloak. The card read: MR. CLAWHAND,  PRESIDENT OF THE LEAGUE OF WORLD SUPERVILLAINS (AND OTHER MEAN PEOPLE).

"It would be a shame to see all your hard work go to waste," he said. His pincer retrieved the kitty-tron from the trash. "You shouldn't be doing fetch quests for milk or playing crossing guard with grannies. There's a far better use for your talent. Something in my field of work, perhaps?"

Tina glanced at the kitty-tron, then back to the business card. She slowly began to realize what Mr. Clawhand was suggesting. "You want me . . . to become Awesome Dog's supervillain?"

"Think of it more like being coworkers," said Mr. Clawhand. "Why sit on the sidelines when you can be part of the action? This is every Awesome Dog fan's dream job. You get to hang out one-on-one with your favorite hero, go on trips together, and occasionally have a bazooka fight. Ya know, typical best-friend stuff."

Tina's eyes lit up. Her heart fluttered. She could

see herself holding Fives by the paw. They were prancing through a field of tulips. Birds chirped in the trees. In the clouds, a plane did loop-the-loops, skywriting *A + T*. A French accordion player wandered in, playing a romantic song. Tina and Awesome Dog each pulled out a bazooka. They clinked the barrels together in a cheers. It was a beautiful moment between best friends. Tina gave Awesome Dog a big kiss on his forehead and said, "I love you."

Mr. Clawhand replied, "Um, what?"

Tina snapped back to reality. She was in the

alley again, holding Mr. Clawhand by his pincer. He had a kiss mark on his forehead.

"Sorry," said Tina. She let go of Mr. Clawhand. "I meant to say, 'I love your idea.' So, what's the first step in becoming a supervillain?"

"It's simple," he said. "Do something bad."

CHAPTER 11

Video Game Reset

MARTY, SKYLER, AND RALPH took their "Get Anything You Want for Free" coupon to the video game store. After weeks of anticipation, *Sheriff Turbo-Karate 2: Gold Deluxe Edition* would finally be theirs.

Skyler skipped down the sidewalk and yelled, "GIDDYUP, PARTNERS! WE'RE GOING TO KICK SOME ALIEN SLIME NINJA BUTT!"

Ralph pretended to ride an invisible horse as he sang a made-up song:

"Hey there, guys and gals!
Wanna play a game with pals?
Sheriff T-K's the way to go!
Gold deluxe is the best fo' sho!
Do a chop with your fist or kick with a boot!
Do a secret code and you'll even toot!"

"Nice dance moves, Ralph," said Skyler.

"Thanks!" he replied. "This morning, I memorized a library book called *The History of International Goofy Dances*. Thought I'd try some out."

The kids arrived at the video game store.

Marty grabbed the door handle and said, "I cannot wrap my noodle around the fact we're about to get *Sheriff Turbo-Karate 2: Gold Deluxe Edition*. Zeroes Club, once we walk through these doors, our lives are going to change forever."

They entered to see that all the shelves were bare. The carpet was covered in mounds of plastic confetti. A pair of police officers was talking to Kev, the store employee.

"Did the security cameras record what happened?" asked one of the cops.

"Yeah. The tape shows that a cat burglar did it," answered Kev.

"Can you give us a description of the thief?" asked the other officer.

Kev scowled and said, "I just did. It was a cat who was a burglar. I think it was some kind of robot, too. It crashed in, stole all the money, and then sliced up all the games with its claws. It's a shame. We're not getting another shipment of *Sheriff Turbo-Karate 2* for three weeks."

"THREE WEEKS!" Ralph cried out. His glasses popped off his face when he heard the bad news.

The cop's shoulder radio crackled. "Attention, all units," the dispatcher said. "There's been a report of a robbery at the Townville Jewelry Store. A robot cat has stolen a giant diamond. The suspect was last seen heading west on Maple Street."

As the cops hurried out of the store, one officer said to the other, "This is the ninth robbery today."

"Where's Awesome Dog when you need him?" asked his partner.

"It's time to suit up, Team Awesome," said Marty, balling up his fists. "Nobody messes with our video games!"

CHAPTER 12

Dog Chases Cat

TO BECOME AWESOME DOG'S ultimate supervillain (and hopefully get an autograph),

Tina had taken Mr. Clawhand's advice and done something bad. Actually, she'd done a lot of bad, all over Townville.

Tina was normally a very good person, but her increasing obsession with Awesome Dog had made her anything but normal. Her mind had twisted to the point where she was no longer thinking straight. She now had one goal: to get Awesome Dog to notice her by any means possible.

After upgrading her robot cat with a sturdier

body, Tina had reprogrammed it to stop helping the neighborhood and instead wreck it. Kitty-tron 2000 robbed and smashed up shops, banks, and museums all over Townville.

She knew committing so many crimes would catch the attention of Team Awesome, and her scheme had paid off when the kitty-tron hit the video game store. Next, there would

be a big battle. Team Awesome would be so impressed with her robot cat's amazing bad-guy skills that they'd crown Tina their ultimate supervillain, and they'd all become best friends forever.

Or so Tina had dreamed up in her head. This is what really happened. . . .

"BARK. BARK. INTERCEPTING TARGET IN FIVE THOUSAND FEET," said Awesome Dog.

Team Awesome had jetted downtown on Awesome Dog's leash to catch the kitty-tron. They had spotted it crawling up a skyscraper. It had the stolen diamond in its mouth.

Marty clicked on the Funstation's heads-up display. "Fives, what're we up against?"

Awesome Dog's ears transformed into satellites. They scanned the target. "BARK. BARK. CLASS TWO CYBERNETIC MECH-BOT. POTENTIAL THREATS: RAZOR CLAWS, CLAMPING TEETH, HIGH-SPEED YARN BALL SHOOTER. BAD ATTITUDE."

"Could be dangerous," said Skyler. "Let's keep our distance and take it out with a sneak attack."

"Not sure I agree with you," said Ralph. "A direct hit from Awesome Dog's missile will wipe

it out completely. We need to capture it so we can figure out what it is."

Marty considered the two approaches. Blast or capture. It was a tough decision. "All right. Fives, get in close and be ready to fire," ordered Marty.

Awesome Dog swooped forward and flew vertically up the side of the building. His mega-cannon popped out. His eyes switched to crosshairs. "BARK. BARK. LOCKED ON TARGET."

Marty slightly adjusted Fives's aim on the controller and pressed the "C" button. Awesome Dog's cannon fired. The missile skimmed over the kitty-tron's head, but Marty hadn't missed. The missile struck the building's ledge. The explosion broke free a gargoyle. The statue dropped off and smacked Kitty-tron 2000 square in the nose. The robot cat flailed backward off the building. It dropped fifty stories and cratered into the sidewalk.

"Thought we could do a *light* sneak attack," said Marty. "And ask questions afterward."

CHAPTER 13

Best Friends For-never

AWESOME DOG LANDED next to the smashed kitty-tron on the pavement. The cat's body was busted and smoldering from the fall off the building. It stood up in a wobbled stance. The stolen diamond dropped out of its broken jaw.

"MEOW. M-M-MEOW," the kitty-tron glitched. "SYSTEMS CRITICAL. MISSION FAILURE. ANYONE ELSE SMELL BURNT P-P-PANCAKES?"

Ralph asked, "What is your mission?"

"TO BE YOUR ULTIMATE SUPERVILLAIN!" it answered.

Kitty-tron 2000 leapt at Ralph with its claws out. Ralph was caught off guard and panicked. He stumbled backward, tripping over his own feet. The kitty-tron dove in, swiping its claws and—

It was blown to bits. Awesome Dog had auto-fired his mega-cannon to save Ralph. There was an eruption of applause. An audience had gathered to see the chase.

"Nice job, Awesome Dog!" said a business-man.

"Mad pilot skills, Super Awesome!" shouted Granny Nunchucks.

"Purple Lightning, you're cooler than my mom!" yelled a two-year-old boy.

Everyone on Team Awesome was being celebrated—everyone except Ralph. No one was cheering his name. While his friends were stand-

ing tall and brave, Ralph was on his backside. He got to his feet with a heavy sigh. He had blown his chance to be a hero once again.

"Your dog is so . . . AWESOME! He's Dawgsome!" said Tina. She had also been watching from the street and was bursting with giddiness.

She was setting herself up for their big introduction. "That robot cat was probably, like, the most ultimate supervillain you've ever met, though, am I right?"

"BARK. BARK. ENEMY HAS FAILED TO QUALIFY AS SUPERVILLAIN. NOT SUPER ENOUGH. TOO EASY," said Awesome Dog.

Skyler picked up a few metal scraps off the sidewalk and dunked them into a trash can. "We turned that cat into kitty litter!"

KITTY-DUNK!

All the spectators laughed. Tina was nudged aside as the crowd rallied around the kids, chanting, "AWE-SOME! AWE-SOME! AWE-SOME!"

This wasn't at all how Tina had expected

the fight to end. Her
eyebrows scrunched
together in confu-
sion. The excitement
drained from her face,
which then filled with
frustrated anger. As
she turned to leave,
she noticed a blinking
light on the ground. A
single flea-tron had
survived the kitty-
tron explosion. She
picked it up from the
sidewalk.

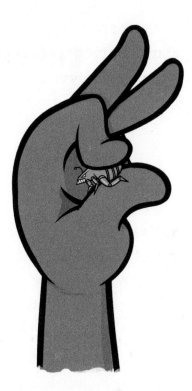

Tina's keen intellect began formulating a new
plan to become Awesome Dog's ultimate supervillain. It was far more sinister than the first
plan. She whispered orders to the tiny flea-tron,
and it bounded off on its mission.

Team Awesome gave a wave to their fans before rocketing off to return the diamond to the
jewelry store. Tina smirked as they soared away.
"Okay, Team Awesome. I'll show you something
super."

CHAPTER 14

Rookie Mistakes

WITH ALL THE COPIES OF *Sheriff Turbo-Karate 2* sliced and diced, Team Awesome would have to wait nearly a month to get a new one. They were upset, but the kids still had another game they could play. Marty, Skyler, and Ralph had signed up for the Nikola Tesla Elementary basketball team, and they were having their first practice in the gym.

Coach Pumpiron blew the whistle around his

neck. The big, hulking guy was in his usual tight shorts and visor. He shouted, "Take a knee!"

Ralph grabbed the middle of his pant leg.

"No, it means get down on one knee," said Marty.

Ralph quickly knelt with the other kids. The mix-up was understandable. Ralph had never played sports. He would much rather have spent the afternoon reading the inventor's journal again, but he wanted to hang out with his friends.

Coach Pumpiron crossed his arms. "We've got our first game against Thomas Edison Elementary coming up soon," he said. "So today we're going over fundamentals. Let's get started!"

The kids lined up to practice dribbling. Each player was to take the ball to the half-court line and back. Marty went first. He dribbled

down the court, then did a crossover, spun around, and returned with ease. If Marty had style, Skyler had speed. She sprinted with the ball to the line and was back in two squeaks of her sneakers.

Then Ralph was up. He slapped the ball up and down as he waddled sideways, awkwardly bent over so that his butt stuck out. There was a

snicker from one of the other players. It was the leader of the cool kids, Shades.

"Check out this dork!" he said. "Ralph dribbles like a duck with a wedgie!"

Ralph's feelings were hurt, but he pretended not to hear the comment. He finished dribbling and got back to the line without saying anything. The kids started their next drill, passing.

Coach Pumpiron partnered everyone up. They were to stand ten feet apart and toss the ball back and forth. Ralph was paired with Skyler. He took a deep breath, visualized the pass in his mind, and threw. The ball got a solid bounce, and Skyler caught it. Ralph's eyebrows popped up in surprise. He couldn't believe it. He'd made the pass!

Then Skyler tossed the ball back. Ralph

reached out but fumbled the catch. When he'd stepped forward to grab it, he'd accidentally booted it away. He couldn't believe it. He'd messed up the pass!

"This isn't soccer, Ralph," said Coach Pumpiron. "Hands only."

"Funny you should mention that," said Ralph. "Fun fact! In 1891, basketball was originally played with a soccer ball and peach baskets."

Coach Pumpiron stared at Ralph for a moment. Then he said, "This isn't 1891, either, kid. Don't kick the ball."

All the players assembled near the free-throw line for the shooting drill. Marty stepped forward, squared up, and shot the ball. It swished in.

Ralph was next. He was given a ball and eyed

the basket. It seemed miles away. Ralph jumped up as high as he could before releasing the shot. It soared through the air . . .

And flew over the basket, through the open gym door, and into the hallway. There was the sound of shattering glass.

A custodian yelled, "HEY! WHO THREW THAT BALL!"

Shades joked, "Oh no! This gym is getting soooo dangerous! We need Awesome Dog to come save us before Ralph shoots again!"

All the cool kids laughed. Ralph's shoulders slumped. A gloomy frown dropped over his face.

Skyler tried to cheer him up. "Don't listen to them, Ralph," she said. "You're doing fine. It's called practice for a reason. We're here to get better."

Coach Pumpiron blew another whistle, and Skyler jogged off for the next drill. When she took her place in line, Marty asked her, "Where'd Ralph go?"

They both turned to see the exit door closing. Ralph was gone.

CHAPTER 15

Uninvited Guests

WHEN RALPH GOT OFF THE HQ0 elevator, Awesome Dog was there to greet him with his antenna tail wagging.

"BARK. BARK. HELLO, RALPH," said Awesome Dog. "I HAVE MISSED YOU!"

Ralph walked past Awesome Dog. He was feeling down after quitting on basketball practice. "Thanks, Fives, but I don't want to play. I'm not in the mood."

"BARK. BARK. MOOD-IMPROVEMENT PROGRAM ACTIVATED!" said Fives. He scratched behind his ear and followed Ralph. "BARK. BARK. PLEASE SELECT ONE OF MY FUN ENTERTAINMENT PROGRAMS: GOING FOR A WALK, FETCH, HIDE-AND-SEEK, CHECKERS, BAKING COOKIES, OR BLOWING UP THINGS WITH A MISSILE."

Ralph laughed. Awesome Dog had made him feel better with the choices. Ralph decided to set up the checkers board. Awesome Dog went first. He used his paw to slide a red piece forward. He scratched behind his ear again.

"Why are you so itchy, Fives?" asked Ralph. He examined Awesome Dog's head. Ralph plucked off a tiny speck. It was a flea-tron.

DING! The elevator bell rang. The doors parted

to reveal two figures inside. Ralph called out, "Marty, Skyler, you got to see this!"

"Oh, I already know what it is," said Tina Tinkerwith. "It's the tracking device that led me here."

Tina stepped out of the elevator in a fancy new supervillain outfit. She was draped in a long, shimmering silver coat with matching neon-green gloves and knee-high boots. Her mask extended up like two animal ears.

She looked over the room and gushed, "Oh my gadgets! Can I just say I love what you've done with the space. It's got this high-tech secret lab feel mixed with a cozy treehouse vibe."

"Hey! You're not allowed to be down here, ma'am!" said Ralph.

"'Ma'am'? Pffft. Please, that's way too formal. You can call me Lady Catastrophe!" said Tina. She twisted at the waist to show off the cat face on the back of her jacket. "Emphasis on the C-A-T. Whaddya think? I was considering doing the outline in neon lights, but it seemed a tad much, and I didn't want to look like I was trying too hard to impress you. I mean, I did—*do*—want to impress you because I'm, like, your biggest fan. Am I talking too much? It feels like I'm talking too much. Whew. Sorry. I ramble when I get a lot of nervous energy built up. I'm new to this whole ultimate-supervillain thing."

Ralph realized who she was. "It was *your* robot cat we blew up."

"Well, you blew up one of them," corrected Tina. She snapped her fingers. From out of the elevator, a robot cat galloped in. Its body was much more refined than previous versions', constructed of sleek hardened steel, with a heavy tail. The cat's claws were longer and sharper. The shape of its triangular eyes made the cat look like it was constantly scowling, and its teeth formed a big shark-tooth grin. It was Kitty-tron 3000.

"Ralph Rogers," said Tina, "we have a lot to talk about."

CHAPTER 16

Bad Kitty

LADY CATASTROPHE NODDED to the tiny robot between Ralph's fingers. "A little bug told me *alllll* about you and Marty Fontana and Skyler Kwon," she said.

Kitty-tron 3000 slunk in and around Lady Catastrophe's legs before heeling at her side. She petted the cat behind its ear. The kitty-tron let out a *purrrr* as loud as a racecar revving up.

"As you can see, I've made a few minor enhancements since our skyscraper battle," said

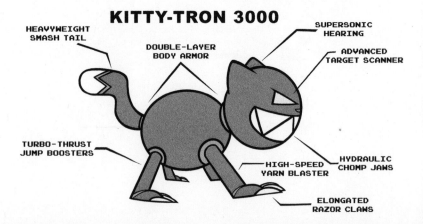

KITTY-TRON 3000

HEAVYWEIGHT
SMASH TAIL

DOUBLE-LAYER
BODY ARMOR

SUPERSONIC
HEARING

ADVANCED
TARGET SCANNER

TURBO-THRUST
JUMP BOOSTERS

HIGH-SPEED
YARN BLASTER

HYDRAULIC
CHOMP JAWS

ELONGATED
RAZOR CLAWS

Lady Catastrophe. "I knew I'd need some heavy firepower for our big showdown at the—oh. Uh, spoiler alert! I'm getting ahead of myself. I've put together a very intricate master plan for us, and I wouldn't want to ruin any of the surprises for Mr. Cutesy-Wootsy over here. May I pet him?"

She raised her hand toward Awesome Dog. The mega-cannon popped out of Fives's back. He steadied his aim, and his eyes switched to cross-hairs.

"Now, really? Is that any way to treat a fan?" asked Lady Catastrophe.

She pointed at Awesome Dog. Her new glove had a special targeting laser in the index finger. A red dot appeared on Fives's cannon.

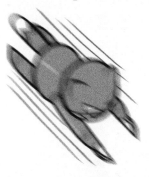

In a blur of silver, Kitty-Tron 3000 claw-sliced the weapon clean off. Then the robot cat swung its tail. Awesome Dog

was smacked hard against the snout. He flopped sideways to the floor.

Ralph ran over to protect Fives. This was Ralph's moment to prove his bravery. He picked up his superhero ski mask and pulled it over his face. He stood tall, defiant. He wasn't going to cower in fear this time. Ralph reached into his hoodie and attached his custom Fun-station to Fives's leash.

"Fun fact!" he said. "Greyhounds are the world's fastest dog breed—not counting robot dogs, of course."

Ralph mashed the "A" button. Awesome Dog's rocket paws ignited. They both shot forward at one hundred miles an hour to ram Lady Catastrophe, but Kitty-tron 3000's programming had anticipated the attack. The robot cat dove to the side and fired high-speed yarn balls back at Awesome Dog.

Ralph wasn't as good at piloting as Marty or Skyler. He couldn't dodge the shots. Awesome Dog took the hits and veered right into HQ0's wall of televisions.

Awesome Dog was shaking the dizzy out of his head when Kitty-tron 3000 pounced on top of him. Its claws stabbed into Awesome Dog's sides. It lifted Fives up and body-slammed him. The robot cat clamped Fives's paws to the floor.

Kitty-tron 3000 flashed its fangs. "MEOW. MEOW. CAN I DESTROY THE TARGET?"

"Destroy?! Absolutely not!" Lady Catastrophe said with a scowl. Then a smile crept across her face. "That happens much, much later. This is the part where the super-villain and the superhero meet properly for the first time. I demonstrate how powerful I am, humiliate the heroes, leave them without any hope of victory, and start the final stages of my master plan."

"You'll never get away with this," said Ralph.

Lady Catastrophe rolled up his ski mask, exposing Ralph's face. "I guess you're going to have to try and stop me, then, Professor I.Q." She gave a wink and laser-pointed her finger at Ralph's forehead. "But do try a little harder next time."

POP! Ralph was smacked with a yarn ball from Kitty-tron 3000. It was an instant knockout.

CHAPTER 17

A Catastrophic Failure

RALPH WOKE UP TO FIND Awesome Dog licking his cheek. Marty and Skyler were standing over him.

"What happened here?" asked Marty.

Ralph sat up. He grimaced when he saw Awesome Dog. The kitty-tron attack had left his friend in terrible shape. He was covered in dents and scrapes. His sides were cut with two deep slashes.

"This is all my fault. I couldn't stop her," said Ralph.

"Couldn't stop who?" asked Skyler.

"BARK. BARK. ACCESSING CAMERA PLAYBACK," said Awesome Dog. His eyes projected a video replay onto the wall.

"*You can call me Lady Catastrophe,*" the video said. "*Emphasis on the C-A-T.*"

The kids watched as the kitty-tron beat up Fives, Lady Catastrophe explained her plan, and Ralph got struck with the yarn ball.

"BARK. BARK. PLAYBACK COMPLETE," Awesome Dog said.

"Ralph, this isn't your fault," said Skyler. "That lady's new robot is a terminator kitty. You did your best to stop her."

"My best?!" asked Ralph. He shook his head. All his frustration came flooding out. "My best is never good enough. You and Marty are so great

at all this, and I keep failing over and over again. Marty, when you put on your superhero costume, you look like a real superhero. And, Skyler, how you spoke at the mayor's event—you're a natural leader. I try to stop a villain on my own, and I end up crashing Fives and getting a face full of yarn. You two are cool and strong and fast and brave. And I'm just . . . different." Ralph sniffled and wiped the corner of his eye. "I can't even make the basketball team. Do you really think I belong on a team of superheroes?"

Marty took a moment to process what Ralph had said. After he thought it over, he said, "Yeah. You're right, Ralph. You are different."

Ralph raised an eyebrow in confusion. That was not the response he'd been expecting. But Marty wasn't finished yet. "And that's why you *do* belong on this team, Ralph. Our differences make us stronger."

"How could being bad at something be good?" asked Ralph.

"It's like this," said Skyler. She sat down next to him. "Do you remember how to defeat the asteroid boss in the first *Sheriff Turbo-Karate* game?"

"Yeah, of course. You find the Astro-Lobster,

hitch a ride on his spaceship, and do flame kicks," said Ralph.

"Exactly!" said Skyler. "You can't beat the level with just Sheriff Turbo-Karate. He can't fly the ship, and Astro-Lobster can't do flame kicks. But when you team them up, the two combine their unique skills to beat Prince Rocko. You don't have to be the best at everything, Ralph. You just have to be the best at being yourself."

"So, what unique skill do I have that helps this team?" asked Ralph.

Marty tapped his temple. "You're the brains of this operation."

"And we're gonna need 'em," said Skyler. "This upgraded robot cat is an epic problem."

Epic? Ralph thought. He held up a finger and said, "Fun fact! The part of the brain that comes up with new ideas is called the prefrontal cortex." He went to the workbench and grabbed the inventor's journal. He held it up. "We use this to give Awesome Dog some upgrades of our own."

"Ralph, you said it yourself: those blueprints are a bunch of random inventions," said Marty. "How are we supposed to upgrade Awesome Dog with an alarm clock?"

Ralph picked up a pencil and paper and began to sketch out a design. "We can convert the randomness *into* weaponry. I'll need eight hundred pounds of reinforced steel plating, a quad-powered thermal booster, an XRC motherboard, four—no, six—yards of nanowiring—"

Skyler interrupted. "Whoa, whoa, whoa. Ralph, where are we supposed to get all that junk?"

Ralph showed off his finished drawing. It was Awesome Dog with an arrow pointing to a detailed robotic suit. "We go to the junkyard," said Ralph.

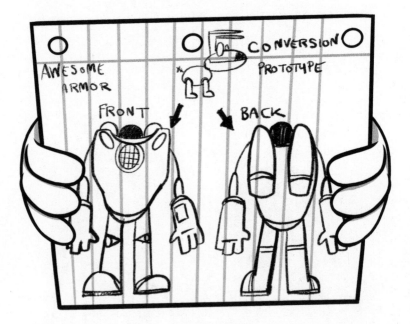

CHAPTER 18

Epic Supply Run

RALPH'S DESIGN WOULD completely over-haul Awesome Dog's build from the inside out, top to bottom. Once applied, Fives could transform his entire body into wearable armor equipped with a unique arsenal. It was a clever concept, but Ralph hadn't come up with it on his own. To stop their new supervillain, he had taken some inspiration from their last one.

The kids flew to the junkyard. It had been the site of their final showdown with Mayor Bossypants a few weeks prior. The battleground had been left untouched. The mayor's monster truck

was still parked off to the side. There were empty bleachers set up for the mayor's fans. Fragmented chunks of metal and electronics were piled up under the magnetic crane. The scraps were the remains of Mayor Bossypants's "epic" giant mech-suit. The kids had come back to recycle the parts.

"As always, smart thinking, Ralph," said Marty. He picked up the mech-suit's detached T-shirt cannon. "There's more than enough stuff here to complete your blueprint for Awesome D—

AAAAAAAAAAAAAH!"

When Marty had lifted up the part, he was shocked to find a small man hiding underneath. He had a scruffy

beard and a tattered suit. It was one of Mayor Bossypants's former assistants, Bird-Watching Teeny.*

"Shoo! Shoo! Get out of here!" said Skyler. She waved the little assistant away. The Teeny let out

---

* Backstory note: He was formerly known as Slideshow Teeny, until he accidentally exposed an embarrassing picture of Mayor Bossypants. We would show this image, but it was so embarrassing that the mayor had the picture banned from ever being displayed in public.**

** Right-now story note: Mayor Bossypants is a bad guy who's in jail,

a *squeak-squeak* before scampering off on all fours like a frightened rat. Abandoned by his boss and left with no purpose in his life, the assistant now slept in a nest of garbage and howled at the moon at night. His new title was Stinky Wildman Teeny.

"Let's gather up these materials and get out of here before any more of those creepy dudes show up," said Ralph.

The kids wrapped Awesome Dog's leash around the scrap pile. They bundled all the parts together and headed back to HQ0. Ralph had an awesome mech-suit to build.

HOOOOOOOOOWL!

so who cares what he thinks. Here's that embarrassing picture and a few others of the mayor just for fun:

CHAPTER 19

Executive Playtime

SHERIFF TURBO-KARATE SPUN through the air in a twisting roundhouse. He yelled, "YEE-HAW!"

He kicked over a colossal mug. Coffee flooded an oversized stapler. The sheriff picked up a pencil as tall as he was. He tossed it in the air and chopped it in half. He then bowed to the giant man holding a remote control.

It wasn't a real giant. It was the normal-sized president of Funstation, Mr. Videomoto. He had been controlling the miniature sheriff doll to kick and punch things on his desk. The company's toy designers had finally created what their boss had always wanted: a non-beach bum, non-lumberjack, non-butterfly man, regular Sheriff Turbo-Karate action figure.

"I am so incredibly happy with this toy!" Mr. Videomoto exclaimed. "Nothing can ruin this perfect day!"

There was a *knock, knock* at the door.

"Excuse me, sir." His secretary popped her head around the office door. "I apologize for interrupting your dolly playtime."

"Ugh!" moaned Mr. Videomoto. "Let me guess. The factory control panel malfunctioned again. How many toys were built incorrectly this time?"

"No. The machines are working fine. There's someone here to see you," said his secretary.

"I'm a little busy right now, but okay, send them in." Mr. Videomoto had just stood up to greet his guest when Kitty-tron 3000 slashed the

door apart. The robot cat rushed in and fired two yarn balls directly into Mr. Videomoto's gut. He doubled over and dropped to his knees.

Lady Catastrophe strutted into the office. "Sorry. I probably should have made an appointment, but I really wanted to see you right away about getting a job."

"Tina? Tina Tinkerwith? Is that you?" asked Mr. Videomoto. He barely recognized her in the costume. "You just sucker-punched me with a yarn fastball. Why would I ever rehire you as a toy designer?"

"No. No. No. I don't want that little job anymore. I'm here for *your* job. I'm taking over as the new president of Funstation," said Lady Catastrophe.

She rounded Mr. Videomoto's desk and took a seat. She picked up the Sheriff Turbo-Karate doll and studied the craftsmanship.

"This is unbelievable," said Lady Catastrophe.

"Thank you," said Mr. Videomoto.

"Unbelievably boring. Trash it!" she yelled. She tossed it over to her kitty-tron. Its claws diced the action figure into sheriff strips and chowed down on the pieces. Tina gave a sly grin and said, "We're going to make some new toys!"

CHAPTER 20

The Awesome Armor

AWESOME DOG STARED UP AT Marty and
Skyler with his tongue
hanging out the side
of his mouth.

"This is it?" asked
Skyler. "He's exactly
the same. I thought
you were going to give
him some tricked-out
mech-armor, Ralph."

Ralph's hoodie was stained with oil marks.
Machine parts and tools were littered across the
floor of HQ0. He had worked all afternoon re-
building Fives and was ready to show off the results. He placed a shoestring necklace on Marty.
It had a small, slender whistle at the end.

"This is the key," explained Ralph.

Marty blew into the whistle. Nothing happened. "It doesn't work," he said.

"The sound's too high-pitched for humans to hear," said Ralph. "It's a dog whistle. You might want to stick out your arms a little."

Ralph lifted Marty's arms up at his sides into a T-pose. Awesome Dog's eyes started blinking. The whistle had engaged his upgrade.

"BARK. BARK. AWESOME ARMOR ACTIVATED."

Suddenly, Fives jumped into an aerial somersault toward Marty. Awesome Dog's whole body reconfigured itself in midair and began transforming. His chest and back legs split open. His head retracted. His eyes and nose transformed into a high-tech mask. His front legs converted

into a twin-jet backpack. All of Awesome Dog's components wrapped around Marty, encasing him in a robotic suit.

Marty's eyes went wide. He couldn't believe what he was wearing.

He stood frozen in silence. He was so still and quiet, you could hear him blink.

Skyler burst out at the top of her lungs, "WHAT?!?!?!?!?!?!?!?!" She ran over to Ralph and started shaking him by the shoulders. She yelled out her words one by one:

"RALPH! THIS! IS! THE! COOLEST! THING! EVER! IN THE ENTIRE HISTORY OF THE UNIVERSE!"

The speaker on the Awesome Armor's chest sounded: "BARK. BARK. READY FOR BATTLE." Fives's body might have changed, but his mind was still intact.

"Oh yeah, we're ready for battle!" said Skyler. "Let's get some target practice going. Awesome Dog, pop out your mega-cannon."

"BARK. BARK. COMMAND ERROR," said Fives's speaker.

She tried again. "Fives, activate mega-cannon."

"BARK. BARK. COMMAND ERROR."

"Quit saying 'command error' and just open the thingy. . . . Where is the thingy?" asked Skyler. She searched over the armor for the hatch.

"I ditched the mega-cannon and all the ammo," said Ralph. "With Fives carrying a person, and the thicker armor, I needed to keep the rig as light as possible for maximum speed. That's also why Marty's the only one who can fit into the suit."

"Yes! I knew being short was going to come in handy one of these days," said Marty.

"Okay, so if you took out the mega-cannon, what'd you replace it with?" asked Skyler.

Ralph adjusted his glasses with a grin. "Awesome Dog, activate weapons tutorial."

CHAPTER 21

All Dressed Up and Ready to Go

RALPH HAD USED the inventor's journal to create dozens of features for the Awesome Armor's defense. It was waterproof, more durable, antimagnetic, and even odor-resistant. The built-in air freshener would keep it from getting too stinky when Marty sweated. There's nothing worse than the smell of wet dog. The biggest improvements, however, were to the armor's offense.

DEFENSE +++   ATTACK

Ralph had taken the plan for the inventor's grappling-hook pen and adapted it into a whip. With a simple flick of the wrist, Awesome Dog's leash would unspool from the suit's right hand. The whip could be used for lassoing baddies or doing a Tarzan swing from a branch.

"Try it out," said Ralph. "Get yourself a juice box."

Marty slung his hand toward the mini-fridge in the corner. The whip shot out and grabbed the door handle. Marty jerked his hand back. Instead of opening the door, the entire fridge was yanked and smashed into the wall across the room. Fruit punch splashed everywhere.

"I wasn't thirsty anyway," said Marty.

Ralph's second alteration was to the over-powered alarm clock. He had redesigned it into a supersonic bark attack. Instead of a wake-up call, the armor's speaker would release a shock-wave. The closer the target was to the speaker, the stronger the attack.

"The bark uses a massive amount of con-centrated energy. So it can't be used a lot, or it will overload the circuitry," said Ralph. "But it shouldn't be a problem. One shot ought to do the trick."

Skyler volunteered to help test it. She strapped on her helmet and put in earplugs. Ralph had

wrapped her body in so many layers of Bubble Wrap, she looked like a plastic snowman.

Ralph stood behind Marty. He called out, "You good, Skyler?" She squeezed her hand through a gap in the wrapping and gave a thumbs-up. Marty closed his eyes and stuck out his chest. The suit's speaker roared.

Even thirty feet away, the blast was strong enough to knock Skyler off her feet. She pinballed around the room. Her protective Bubble Wrap *snapped! popped! popped! snapped! popped!* with each bounce. Skyler rolled to a stop

and fell out of the plastic. She had a big smile on her face. "Wooo-wee! I guess we won't be using that one in the library."

Ralph didn't have to modify the blueprint for the third weapon. It was powerful enough on its own. "This one's for a worst-case scenario," warned Ralph. "If we get into a situation where all options have failed, then and only then do we use this."

Ralph pressed a button on Marty's left forearm. A hidden compartment slid open. Inside was a single black pod the size of a golf ball.

"It's a black hole space-grenade," said Ralph. "The journal's blueprint said it consumes everything into darkness. You throw it, and it explodes on impact."

"Are we sure it's safe for us to use black holes?" asked Marty. "This seems really advanced for fifth graders. I mean, I don't even know how to work a laundry machine."

"Like I said, it's a last resort against Lady Catastrophe," said Ralph.

"Speaking of, how are we supposed to find Ms. Ultimate Supervillain?" asked Skyler.

Marty used the leash whip to grab the TV remote. He pulled it back into his hand and clicked on one of the console's TV screens that Fives's *hadn't* crashed into.

"If Lady Catastrophe has a master plan, she isn't going to be shy about it," said Marty.

He flipped through the channels until he found a news show. It was in the middle of a report: ". . . has the mayor worried. Every time the police have tried to enter the building, they've been smacked in the face with balls of yarn. It appears the Funstation toy factory has been hijacked, and all the employees have been fired. The culprits are a mysterious woman in a very fashionable outfit

and a robot kitty. She's made only a single state-ment of her intent—and I quote: 'In one hour, I will reveal the true identity of all three costumed members of Team Awesome.' Why she would do that is kind of weird, but I guess we should be happy she's not trying to take over the world."

"If we go to the factory, we'll be falling right into her trap," said Skyler.

"What do you think, Ralph?" asked Marty.

Ralph pondered the possible options for the team. Then he said, "Technically, it's not a trap if we know it's a trap, right?"

"Awesome Dog, deactivate armor," said Marty. The mech-suit removed itself as it transformed back into Fives's normal dog form. "Looks like we're going for a walk."

CHAPTER 22

The Funstation Factory Fight

AWESOME DOG SOARED through the open window of the Funstation president's office. He was towing the kids on his leash. They all landed in front of the boss's desk. Lady Catastrophe was seated behind it with Kitty-tron 3000 resting in her lap.

"All right! I'm so glad you made it!" she said, and checked her watch. "I was starting to get worried I'd have to spill your little secret. Which I totally would never do, by the way. That's far too mean. I hope you're not mad, but I only said it to get you here to force you into a big rematch."

"There's not going to be a rematch, Lady Catastrophe," said Marty. "You're going to surrender the factory, give back all the stuff you stole, and—are you taking a selfie?"

Lady Catastrophe was holding her phone up with her back to the kids. CLICK! There was a flash as the photo snapped. She spun around and said, "I needed something to remember this moment. I absolutely love everything about Team Awesome!"

"Being a supervillain is a funny way of showing your affection," said Skyler.

"To be the best superhero team possible, you need someone to challenge you," said Lady Catastrophe. "It's called tough love."

She snapped her fingers. In a flash, Kitty-tron 3000 leapt over the desk and swung its tail at Awesome Dog. Fives ducked, and the cat whiffed.

"See! You're already showing improvement from our last battle," said Lady Catastrophe.

"I'll show you an improvement," said Marty. He blew the dog whistle around his neck.

"BARK. BARK. AWESOME ARMOR ACTIVATED," said Awesome Dog. He did a backflip and changed into the mech-suit, instantly covering Marty.

Lady Catastrophe shot up from her seat and exclaimed, "Is this for real?! I mean, I knew you'd come up with a way to stop me, but this is like . . . like . . . MAXIMUM WOWAGE! Turning Awesome Dog into clothes is a fierce choice!"

Her compliments were making Marty angry. She wasn't taking this seriously. He made two fists and clenched his jaw as he glared at Lady Catastrophe.

She asked, "Are you making that face because you need to go to the bathroom, or are we about to start our boss fight?"

Marty slung his hand. The leash whip-lassoed the kitty-tron's right leg. He flung the cat out the window.

Lady Catastrophe gave a nod. "Yep. Definitely the boss fight."

Kitty-tron 3000 jumped back into the office, firing its paw blasters. Marty was pelted with high-speed yarn balls. He stumbled backward, off balance. The robot cat charged in with a claw swipe. Marty shielded himself with his forearms as he was pummeled with a flurry of scratches.

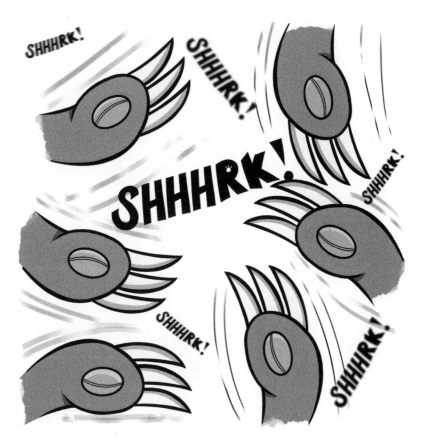

The Awesome Armor was tough, but the slices were cutting deeper and deeper. Marty had to stop the cat before it tore the suit apart. He took a step back, opened his arms up, and unleashed a supersonic

The shockwave threw the kitty-tron backward into the wall, where the robot cat shattered into metal shards. The blast threw Marty in the

opposite direction, out of the office, and down three flights of stairs.

Skyler and Ralph rushed after him and helped him up. The kids found themselves on the main floor of the toy factory. There were rows of machine assembly lines where Sheriff Turbo-Karate dolls were mass-produced.

Lady Catastrophe strolled downstairs and asked, "Are you okay? Your new armor took some nasty scrapes."

"It's going to take more than one robot cat to stop us," said Marty.

"I know," said Lady Catastrophe. "That's why I brought a whole lot more to the fight!"

She pulled out her handheld gizmo and clicked a button. All the factory assembly lines came to life. The conveyor belts rolled forward. Chutes dropped out hollow cat bodies. Auto-mated arms installed circuit boards and con-

nected wiring. Kitty legs and tails were attached. At the last stop, the robot cat heads were screwed on. In mere seconds, the factory had built Lady Catastrophe an army.

She extended her arms wide and said, "I present to you the Kitty-Cat Cyber Squad!"

CHAPTER 23

The Last Resort

RALPH PULLED THE Funstation control out from his hoodie pocket. The heads-up display highlighted all the kitty-trons in the factory: 100 ENEMIES DETECTED.

Lady Catastrophe pointed her laser finger at Marty. The mob of kitty-trons stalked forward. They crept along the floor and crawled along the walls and ceiling.

"Ralph, Skyler, get behind me," said Marty. "It's about to get loud."

He balled up his fists and fired a

BARK!

But the kitty-trons were far enough away to see the attack coming. They scattered behind factory machines for cover. The shockwave rolled across the factory floor and echoed out in all directions. The kitty-trons started their approach again. Marty fired another

The kitty-trons sidestepped it.

It was juked.

Avoided.

BAR-ACK ACK AHEM

The speaker let out a raspy cough. Awesome Dog said, "SUPERSONIC BARK ON STANDBY. TEN-MINUTE COOLDOWN REQUIRED."

"Marty, you overheated the circuits!" said Ralph. "You won't be able to use the bark for a while."

The kids couldn't wait ten minutes for the weapon to cool down. The Kitty-Cat Cyber Squad was closing in.

"Guys, we need to use the black hole space-grenade," suggested Skyler.

"That's a last resort," said Ralph. "We literally just started the fight."

"Yeah, but if we don't fight back, the start is going to be the end," said Marty. He pulled out the grenade. He reared his arm back and—

Skyler stopped him. "Oh! Oh! Can I do it, please?" she asked. "It's been a dream of mine since I was a kindergartner to annihilate an army of evil robots."

Marty shrugged and handed it over. Skyler threw the grenade into the mass of kitty-trons.

It hit the floor and exploded in darkness. Everything went black. . . .

Black *paint*, that is.

The robot cats were stunned and began slipping around in paint puddles. Marty and Skyler were dumbfounded. They looked at Ralph. He had his palm pressed to his forehead. He let out a long, "Ooooooooooooh. That makes way more sense. I thought it was a spelling mistake."

Ralph had built the grenade exactly as the blueprint instructed. Unfortunately, he had mis-

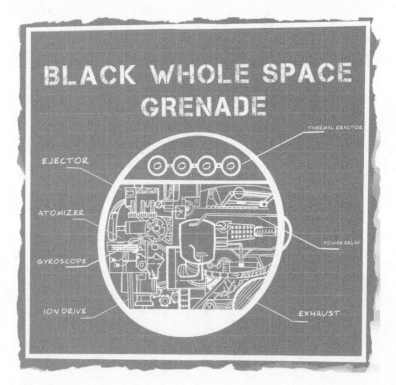

BLACK WHOLE SPACE GRENADE

THERMAL REACTOR

EJECTOR

ATOMIZER

POWER RELAY

GYROSCOPE

ION DRIVE

EXHAUST

read one tiny detail: the name of the weapon. The schematic was not for a "black hole space-grenade," as Ralph had assumed, but rather a "black whole-space grenade." The paint bomb covered an entire area black. It was great for a speedy Halloween decoration, not so great when you were hoping to tear a rift in the cosmos.

"Yeah. That's my bad," said Ralph.

The freshly painted Kitty-Cat Cyber Squad was focused on Marty again. He needed to buy himself some time to think of a way to stop the robot cats. "All right. I guess we're trying out the jetpack," he said. "Awesome Dog, give me max throttle."

"BARK. BARK. ACTIVATE HIGH-SPEED CHASE PROGRAM," said Awesome Dog.

Marty rocketed out the factory's front door. Lady Catastrophe hopped atop two kitty-trons, one for each foot. She stood on the robot cats and commanded her army: "Follow that dog! We can't let him escape! Not without getting an autograph first!"

The Kitty-Cat Cyber Squad robots were the 4000 model, modified with an all-new upgrade.

The kitty-trons began twirling their tails like helicopter propellers. They all took flight after Marty.

CHAPTER 24

Cats Chase Dog

MARTY ZIPPED THROUGH THE city's alleyways with the Kitty-Cat Cyber Squad close behind. He zigzagged, making sharp rights and tight lefts, but the swarm kept on his tail. Lady Catastrophe surfed atop the wave of cats as she

called out, "I see you're playing hard to get . . . and I love it!"

Marty tapped his forearm communicator. "Ralph, do you copy? I can't shake 'em."

Ralph and Skyler were still at the factory. They were monitoring the chase on the Funstation controller. It had a radar display. The little white blip in the middle was Marty. The massive blob of green behind him was the robot cats.

Ralph radioed back, "We copy, Marty. Her robot cats' programming is predicting your flight pattern. You can't outrun them. You'll have to outsmart them."

Marty jetted out onto the main road. There was a giant orange UNDER CONSTRUCTION sign. A crew was repaving the sidewalk. Marty came up with a plan on the fly. He zoomed over and swiped the sign as he passed. He flew low, inches above the ground, and held the sign in front of him at a forty-five-degree angle. He wedged it into the wet concrete as he sped forward. Globs of cement sprayed over the top of the sign and splattered the kitty-trons on his rear. Then he shot up into the clouds.

The kitty-trons gave chase, but after a few seconds they began to slow down. Their propeller tails were acting like fans, quick-drying the moist concrete on their bodies. The robot cats instantly hardened into statues. They plummeted, crashing into one another and shattering as they hit the ground below.

Marty swooped down and landed on the rubble of broken statues. Lady Catastrophe dug herself out of the debris and dusted off her costume.

"You're finished, Lady Catastrophe. Give up," said Marty.

She clutched her chest and gasped. "I would *neeeever* give up on you!" She grabbed her gizmo remote and clicked a button. "I have a master plan to keep this going forever!"

BEEP-BOOP! There was an alert on Marty's forearm computer. The readout showed 100 ENE-MIES DETECTED. He looked in every direction, then tapped his communicator. "Ralph, what's going on?" he asked. "My scanner says there are still kitty-trons, but I don't see any."

Ralph checked his Funstation and replied, "The screen here shows the same thing. It might be a glitch. I'll run a system check."

"It's not a glitch. Lady Catastrophe's cheating," said Skyler. "She's using infinite one-ups."

She pointed at the factory's assembly lines. Lady Catastrophe had remotely started the production of more kitty-trons. New robot cats were

rolling off the conveyor belts and flying away to join the fight.

"Have no fear!" announced Skyler. "Purple Lightning is here, and I'm shutting them down!"

She bolted upstairs to the control booth. Inside, there was a long panel of multicolored buttons, knobs, switches, and levers. The controls were all labeled in Japanese.

"Um," Skyler muttered, "maybe have a little fear. This could be harder than I thought."

CHAPTER 25

Things Get Out of Control

THE FACTORY'S CONTROL PANEL didn't have a simple off switch—at least Skyler couldn't find one. She pushed buttons, flipped levers, and cranked dials. Through the booth's window, she could see that none of her efforts were stopping the assembly lines from making more kitty-trons.

 Clicking one switch would shut down a machine station but speed up two others. One lever activated the fire alarm. Another started the air-conditioning.  A set of switches turned on a hula-girl lamp. There was even a button that flushed the toilet in the adjoining bathroom.

Skyler knew there was only one way to solve the puzzle. She would have to use her tried-and-true method of problem solving.

"Time to smash," she said.

Skyler grabbed the hula-girl lamp and used it to bash the control panel. Buttons and levers broke into pieces. Sparks flickered from the cracks. The assembly lines ground to a halt.

"YES!" exclaimed Ralph. He clicked on his communicator. "Skyler stopped the machines, Marty. There won't be any more kitty-tr—"

Before Ralph could finish telling Marty the good news, the assembly lines started moving again. Skyler hadn't stopped the controls. She had short-circuited them. The machines began to operate erratically. A body frame dropped onto one conveyor belt. Eight legs were bolted onto it. A head was screwed on upside down.

"MEEEEEOW. MEEEEEOW," growled the spider-cat robot.

Another assembly line produced a kitty-tron with an extended neck and four stubby legs. It had made a strange giraffe-cat. One robot was built with a long, narrow body with hundreds of tiny claws for feet: a centipede-cat. Another was only a head with tails for ears. It hopped around like a kitty-rabbit.

Skyler frantically searched the control booth to put a permanent stop to the machines. She

found a cord running from the demolished panel to an outlet on the wall. She pulled it from the socket. It actually was rather easy to shut down the machines. She just had to unplug the control panel.

"Oh," said Skyler.

She had killed the assembly lines, but a horde of freaky robots had already been constructed. The metal monsters shuffled across the factory floor toward Ralph. He sprinted up the stairs and into the control booth to escape. He slammed the door shut. He flicked the lock. He was safe.

Then—

The doorknob jiggled.

The mutant kitty-trons were trying to open the door! There was a low moan. *"MEEEOW. MEEEOW."*

It went eerily quiet.

. . .

THUD! THUD! Two loud bangs struck the door. There was another terrifying *"MEEEOW. MEEEOW."*

Maybe there should be a book warning before this gets too scary.

While this story has been pretty silly so far, these next few chapters are very serious.* These chapters involve intense moments of horror, danger, and freaky robot cats. To prevent readers from developing a fear of regular cats, we've provided the picture below, so you don't forget that most kitties are nice, and all are super cute.

---

* Note: Not too serious, though. There's a fart joke on page 180.

CHAPTER 26

Hot Pursuit

WHILE SKYLER AND RALPH were dealing with a mutant robot invasion, Marty was being chased again. Lady Catastrophe was riding a new wave of one hundred kitty-trons.

Marty weaved through cars toward a busy intersection. The stoplight was red. If Marty didn't pump the brakes, he was going to get obliterated by oncoming traffic.

"BARK. BARK. IMPACT IN TWENTY-FIVE HUNDRED FEET," warned Fives.

Marty checked over his shoulder. The Cyber Squad was gaining distance. It wouldn't be long before they caught him.

"BARK. BARK. MARTY, THERE IS NO CLEAR FLIGHT PATH THROUGH THE INTERSECTION," Fives warned again.

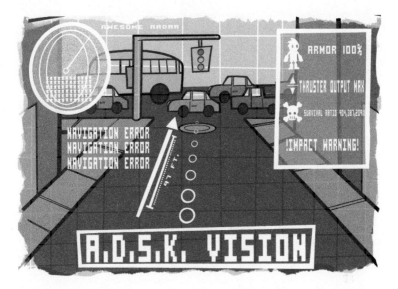

AWESOME RADAR

ARMOR 100%

THRUSTER OUTPUT MAX

SURVIVAL RATIO 904,387,2041

!IMPACT WARNING!

NAVIGATION ERROR
NAVIGATION ERROR
NAVIGATION ERROR

97 FT.

A.D.S.K. VISION

"I'm counting on it," said Marty. He pushed his jetpack harder. It blazed white-hot. The kitty-trons' propellers twirled faster to catch up.

Awesome Dog's sensors tracked the approaching vehicle they were about to hit. It was a large taco truck. "BARK. BARK. WARNING! COLLISION IN . . ."

Marty slung his wrist forward.

"Three . . ."

The leash whip activated and lassoed a manhole cover up ahead.

"Two . . ."

Marty gave a jerk, and the cover popped off.

"One!"

Marty flew into the inter-section and immediately nose-dived into the open sewer.

The Kitty-Cat Cyber Squad was caught off guard by the maneuver. The robot cats over-shot the sewer exit. The swarm barreled into the intersection and plowed into the side of the passing taco truck. It caused a pileup of kitty-trons. There was a massive explosion of robot parts, wires, and com-puter chips.

The taco truck's driver slammed on the brakes. He stumbled out from behind the wheel, holding his face and weeping. Red liquid dripped from his hands. He wasn't hurt. During the crash, a bucket of salsa had spilled on him. He was upset because his delicious taco sauce had been wasted.

Marty jetted out of a manhole a few blocks away from the intersection. He landed on the sidewalk and looked back at the carnage. A thick wall of smoke billowed from the wreckage. One by one, several floating torches lit up in the haze. Marty looked to his forearm computer. The display read: 13 ENEMIES DETECTED. Some of the kitty-trons had survived.

"BARK. BARK. WARNING! INCOMING PROJEC-TILE," said Fives.

Marty looked up. A flaming ball of yarn was coming straight at him. Marty dropped to his stomach as it whizzed past. The last remaining members of the Kitty-Cat Cyber Squad emerged from the crash. Their paws were on fire. With some clever thinking, Lady Catastrophe had

used the grill on the food truck to ignite the sur-
viving pets' blasters.

She glided out on two of her cats. "I think I
may have been going way too easy on you so far.
Maybe my new Kitty-tron 5000s can turn up the
heat!"

The kitty-trons let loose an assault of fiery
yarn balls. It was a rapid-fire attack of . . . well,

rapid fire. Marty took off, spiraling into the sky
as fireballs zoomed around him. He spun and
twirled, but there were too many shots. The Awesome Armor was struck in the back, and Marty
flipped forward. He was whacked in the shoulder
and spun sideways. He was hammered from all

sides. Marty twisted through the air like a burning rag doll. The armor had a lot of defensive features, but fireproofing wasn't one of them.

Marty tried to stabilize himself, but the jetpack was flaming out. The exhaust pipes coughed two puffs of steam before going completely dead. Marty plunged into a free fall. If he didn't do something, he'd be squished onto the city street. Luckily, he spotted a flagpole on top of a nearby building. As Marty dropped, he threw his leash whip and grabbed the pole. He swung back up into the air.

"YES! YES! YES!" cheered Marty.

Then the whip was shot with a yarn fireball. The leash was severed, and Marty started falling again.

"NO! NO! NO!" screamed Marty.

His body dropped through the roof of a store below. Marty was laid out flat on his back. His entire robot suit was charred and smoking. All the customers and employees ran away from what they thought was human toast.

"BARK. BARK. ARMOR

DURABILITY AT THREE PERCENT," said Fives's speaker. "BARK. BARK. WE WILL NOT SURVIVE ANOTHER FIREBALL ATTACK."

Through the hole in the ceiling, Marty could see the kitty-trons circling like vultures. It wouldn't be long before they located him.

Marty rolled his head to the right. There was a rack of T-shirts with Awesome Dog's face on them.

He rolled his head to the left. There was a display of coffee mugs in the shape of Awesome Dog. The store was filled with nothing but Awesome Dog merchandise. There were key chains, plush toys, snow globes, and fridge magnets. Of all the places to suffer a crushing defeat, Marty had dropped into the middle of Fred's Amazing Pup Gift Shop.

"Oh, you've got to be kidding me," groaned Marty.

CHAPTER 27

The Last, Last Resort

"**GRAB A WEAPON, RALPH,**" said Skyler. "There's one exit, and we're going out swinging."

At any moment the robot cat monsters would burst into the control booth and attack them. Ralph scanned the room for a weapon. Anything would work. He found a half-eaten bag of potato chips and three paper clips. Anything would work but those. Ralph checked the booth's bathroom. He returned with a plunger.

"Fun fact! The average person uses the toilet twenty-five hundred times a year," said Ralph.

THUD! THUD! There were two menacing bangs at the locked door.

"Fun fact! There's a myth that Crepitus was the Roman god of farts!" blurted out Ralph.

THUD! THUD! The door started to splinter

down the middle. A few more whacks and the freaky kitty-trons would be inside.

"Fun fact! National Toilet Day is—"

"Ralph!" Skyler stopped him. "Let's chill out on the toilet trivia until we escape the robot nightmare."

Ralph nodded. He gripped his plunger in an attack stance. "Sorry. I'm just scared, Skyler."

"Don't worry, Ralph," said Skyler. Her eyes narrowed as she stared down the door. "I won't let them lay one claw on you."

KA-KRACK! The door was ripped apart. The metal cat monsters poured inside.

Skyler charged at them with her hula-girl lamp. She let out a battle cry: "ALOOOOO-HAAAAAA!!"

Skyler wildly swung the lamp left and right, tearing through the robots. They were freakish in shape but poorly constructed. Skyler threw elbows, jump-kicked, pushed, shoved, and stomped. For her finish move, she ripped the tail-ears off the kitty-rabbit and head-butted it out the door.

When the fight was all over, Skyler stood victorious over the heap of metal scraps. She was panting and sweating. Ralph hadn't moved at all. He was still frozen in fear.

"Fun fact! The average person spends over a year of their life on a toilet," said Ralph. A smile broke over his face. "And now that I'm still alive, I'm looking forward to it."

WHAN-WHAN! WHAN-WHAN! A faint alert sounded from his hoodie. He pulled out his Funstation controller. The screen was flashing multiple warnings.

Ralph clicked on the communicator. "Marty, where are you? What's going on? I'm seeing system failures across the board."

Back in the gift shop, Marty lifted up his right foot. The rocket boot's sole was fried. "I'm grounded, Ralph. The armor's completely off-line."

He tapped on his forearm computer for a status check. The screen showed:

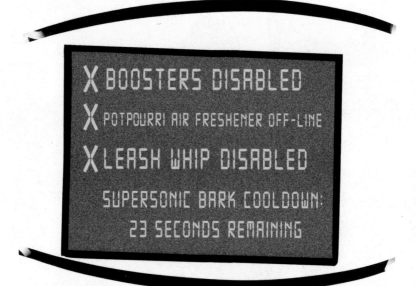

X BOOSTERS DISABLED
X POTPOURRI AIR FRESHENER OFF-LINE
X LEASH WHIP DISABLED
SUPERSONIC BARK COOLDOWN:
23 SECONDS REMAINING

A flea-tron bounced onto the screen. Its alert light blinked red. Marty swatted it into robot bug juice.

"Great. And Lady Catastrophe just found me," said Marty.

"You gotta get out of there fast," said Ralph.

Without his jetpack, Marty would have to make a run for it. He limped through the store toward the exit when something on a shelf caught his eye. Marty smiled and clicked on the communicator. "Ralph, can Awesome Dog use the supersonic bark when he's not in armor form?"

"Yeah, but the moment they see Fives attack, they'll dodge the barks again," said Ralph.

"Who says they'll see it coming?" asked Marty.

CHAPTER 28

Bark with Bite

LADY CATASTROPHE AND HER thirteen kitty-trons converged on Marty's position. They helicoptered down into Fred's Amazing Pup Gift Shop.

Awesome Dog was back in his normal form, sitting next to Marty. Their backs were to a wall of merchandise. If they were going to get beat,

they'd do it together. The kitty-trons crowded in with their flame paws aimed. There was no escape.

"You know the best part of being defeated?" asked Lady Catastrophe, but she didn't wait for an answer. "We'll get to make a sequel together! Aren't you excited?! I'm going to have my kitty-trons completely destroy Awesome Dog! Then you can reassemble him and figure out a whole new strategy on how to stop me again. Only next time we'll have a way bigger showdown. Sequels always take it up a notch. I was thinking we go worldwide! Maybe a battle on an Egyptian pyramid, or a chase along the Great Wall of China, or—no, the Eiffel Tower! Aw! Paris! The City of Love would be perfect for the two of us. It'll be sooooo much fun for me and Awesome Dog fighting forever and ever and ever and ever!"

She pointed her laser finger at Awesome Dog. The kitty-trons shoved Marty away and piled onto Fives. They began tearing at him with their claws. Marty just stood by watching. He didn't say anything.

"What's the matter? Cat got your tongue?" asked Lady Catastrophe.

Marty casually took a pair of Amazing Pup earmuffs off a shelf and put them on. "Not at all," said Marty. "Awesome Dog. Speak."

Lady Catastrophe looked to Awesome Dog. The kitty-trons had shredded him to cotton— *Cotton?* It was a collectible life-sized Amazing Pup stuffed toy! She spun around. The real Awesome Dog was standing directly behind her. Fives let loose a supersonic

BARK!!!

Lady Catastrophe dove behind the checkout register. The Kitty-Cat Cyber Squad was blindsided. At point-blank range, the robot cats absorbed the full force of the speaker's soundwave. They were instantly blasted into dust.

Marty brushed the last of the kitty-trons off his shoulder. He and Awesome Dog went to Lady Catastrophe. She was balled up on the floor with her fingers in her ears.

"It's over. For real this time," said Marty.

Lady Catastrophe shook her head. "No! I'll never surrender!" she said. She reached into her coat pocket and pulled out . . .

A PEN AND PAPER!

"Without getting an autograph first," she said with a grin.

CHAPTER 29

Tesla vs. Edison

TINA TINKERWITH FINALLY got her auto-graph from Awesome Dog. She smooched it nonstop as she walked to the police station and turned herself in. She would get to spend the next twenty years making Awesome Dog col-lages behind bars. It was the happiest she had ever been.

Ralph repaired Awesome Dog, the stolen loot was recovered, and Team Awesome helped fix all the damage to the factory and across the city. Townville celebrated. Their favorite superheroes had saved them again.

The Kitty-Cat Cyber Squad had been defeated, but there was still one more team to face. It was the day of their basketball game, Nikola Tesla Elementary versus Thomas Edison Elementary.

Marty and Skyler took the court with the rest

of the players. They checked the stands. Ralph wasn't there. He had promised his friends he'd show up to support them.

"Maybe he was too embarrassed to come back," said Skyler.

Marty gave a disappointed shrug. "Maybe. C'mon. We've got to get ready for the tip-off."

The game started with a center-court jump ball. Skyler leapt straight up and grabbed the ball. She cut a fast break through defenders and bounce-passed the ball to Marty. He faded back for a jump shot.

SWAT!

A gigantic Edison player slapped it down. He had the number 2 on his jersey. The other team recovered the ball and scored with a layup.

Shades ran up to Marty and said, "I thought you knew how to play, dork. That guy, 2-Tall, just schooled you."

Marty was athletic, but 2-Tall, as Shades called him, was like a fifth-grade basketball pro. Whenever Nikola Tesla had the ball, 2-Tall would take it back. Every pass was stolen. Every shot was blocked. They never got anywhere close to making a basket.

The buzzer sounded. It was halftime. The score was 0–18. If the Nikola Tesla team didn't come up with a way to stop 2-Tall, the game was going to be a shutout. Coach Pumpiron gathered his players into a huddle. "All right, good effort out there, team, but I think it's time we bring in our secret weapon."

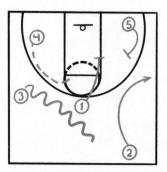

Their coach had never mentioned a secret weapon before. Was it

a trick play? Was it a new player? Was Coach Pumpiron going to blast 2-Tall with a shrink ray?

The buzzer sounded. All the kids were sent back out onto the court without further explanation. Marty brought the ball in for his team. Once again, 2-Tall was there to stop him. Marty tried to spin past him, but 2-Tall threw up his long right arm. Marty pivoted in the other direction. Just as 2-Tall started to raise his left arm, he noticed something on the sidelines.

A lightning bug mascot was high-fiving the air and spanking his own butt. 2-Tall was thoroughly baffled. The distraction gave Marty the perfect opening. He ran in and made a basket. It was a clean *swoosh*.

The lightning bug pulled the mascot head off. It was Ralph. "Nice shot, Marty!" he said.

The Tesla Elementary coach called a time-out, and Marty and Skyler went over to their friend. "Ralph! What're you doing in that ridiculous thing?" Skyler asked.

"I talked to Coach Pumpiron earlier. I know I'm not the best at basketball, but I still wanted to be part of the team," said Ralph. "I asked if I could be the school mascot instead. I figured since I memorized that book on goofy dances, I could bust a move to help out."

Marty loved the game plan. "That's why you're

the brains of the operation, Ralph. You keep dancing, and we'll keep sinking baskets!"

With their new "secret weapon," the Nikola Tesla team was reenergized. On the next play, 2-Tall dribbled downcourt. Ralph let out a "WOOP! WOOP!" to get his attention. Ralph dropped down on all fours and kicked his back legs out like a donkey, and 2-Tall began laughing. Before he realized it, Skyler had swiped the ball and made a basket. Ralph was the perfect distraction for 2-Tall. Ralph did the running man, the sprinkler,

DANCE!

the worm, even the rarely performed electrified hippo, to give his team opportunities to score more points.

The final buzzer sounded. The score was 22–18. Nikola Tesla Elementary had won! In the end, Ralph Rogers, the kid without any athletic ability, had helped the basketball team in his own—and very different—way.

CHAPTER 30

The Paper Trail

MARTY, SKYLER, AND RALPH had each earned their very first basketball trophy. The Zeroes Club brought them down to HQ0, along with the medals they'd gotten from the mayor.

"We're going to need a place to show off all our awards," said Skyler.

"What about over here," said Marty. He went to an empty shelf mounted on the wall. It had been there when the Zeroes first found the secret room. "Little help, Fives?"

The shelf was so high that Marty needed a boost. He used Fives's back as a step stool, and Ralph handed him one of their trophies. Marty stood on his tippy-toes, stretched out his arm, and slid the award onto the shelf. When he did, it pushed off a dusty ball of paper, which fell to the floor.

Skyler uncrumpled it. The paper was a page from a book. Handwritten across the center were these words: *If found please return to owner. The address can be located if you—*

"It's the other half!" said Ralph.

He got the toothbrush inventor's journal and opened it. The front page only had the bottom half. Ralph took the paper from Skyler and matched it up. He read the completed message: "'If found please return to owner. The address

can be located if you just follow the directions.' This must be—"

Skyler cut him off. "Another puzzle?! UGH! Can we for once finish an adventure and *not* have to immediately go on a scavenger hunt?"

"This is our chance to find the inventor of Awesome Dog and learn about the spybots and why he buried a book in the backyard," pleaded Marty.

"Plus, what else are we going to do to pass the time?" asked Ralph. "*Sheriff Turbo-Karate 2: Gold Deluxe Edition* won't be in stores for weeks."

Skyler scrunched her lips to the side. She wasn't so sure. "How are we even supposed to find this toothbrush guy?" she asked. "It says follow the directions, but it's blank. There's nothing else on the page."

"Maybe not on that page," said Ralph. He had read and reread the journal many times, and he remembered seeing little arrows throughout the book. He flipped the pages. "Check it out. Here. Here and here. At the bottom. There are arrows pointing right, down, right."

"'Right, down, right' isn't an address. That's a video game combo move," said Skyler.

"Not if you have a map," said Ralph. He flipped the journal to a mapped grid of Townville. There were thirty boxes, each with a different location in the city. One of them was the inventor's hideout.

"We've got arrows, a map, and a destination," said Marty. He dropped his finger onto the square of the map with his house. "All we have to do is follow the directions."

WANT TO HELP THE ZEROES CLUB FIND THE TOOTHBRUSH INVENTOR?

You can go back to the start of this book and search the bottom of the pages for arrows.

There are thirty chapters, with a single arrow in each one. Ralph gave you a head start by finding the first three. Once you've found the twenty-seven remaining arrows, write the direction they're pointing in—one for each chapter.

After you've found all thirty arrows, you can use them to navigate the map on the next page. Start at the box with Marty's house, labeled START HERE, and move one space at a time in the direction each arrow indicates. If you follow the thirty steps correctly, the path will lead you to the inventor's secret hideout. Then Team Awesome will finally uncover the mystery behind Awesome Dog.

THINK YOU CAN FOLLOW THE DIRECTIONS?

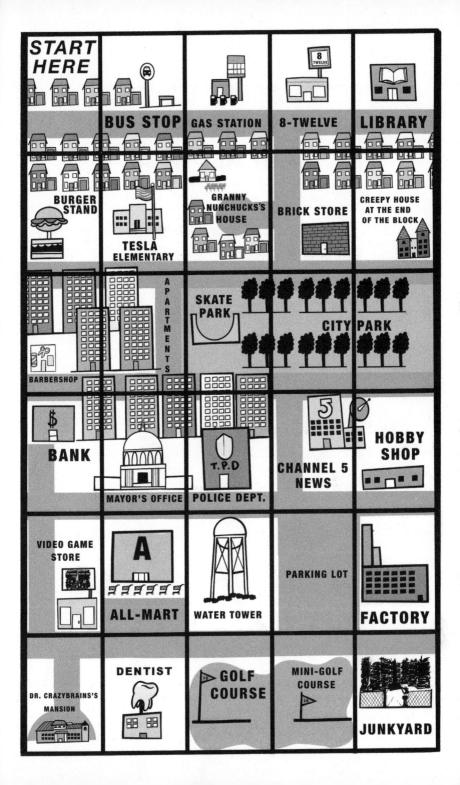

A STARING CONTEST
WITH THIS SNAIL!

The rules are simple. Once someone blinks, they lose. Then turn the page.

BEGIN!

ABOUT THE AUTHOR

Fun fact! Justin Dean is an award-winning writer who's made stuff for television, animation, video games, and now books. When he's not coming up with funny stories, he teaches creative writing to kids. Justin lives in Los Angeles with his wife and two children. Unfortunately, they don't have any robot pets (yet).

[Instagram] @jddean5000
[YouTube] Awesome Draw 5000